Halo
Publishing International

Laurie B Zaring
Jessica Barlup
2013

Illustrated by Jessica Barlup

ISBN 13: 978-1-61244-175-7
Library of Congress Control Number: 2013915298

Printed in the United States of America

Halo
Publishing International
www.halopublishing.com

Published by Halo Publishing International
AP·726
P.O. Box 60326
Houston, Texas 77205
Toll Free 1-877-705-9647
www.halopublishing.com
www.holapublishing.com
e-mail: contact@halopublishing.com

Dedicated with lots of love to our own little animals:
Lexie, Landon, & Lucas Zaring, and Henry Barlup.
Don't ever be afraid to chase your dreams! May your imaginations always run "wild"! ~from your mommies!

TIGERS
MONKEYS
ZEBRAS
ELEPHANTS
BEARS
GIRAFFES
LIONS
POSSIBILITIES...
ZOO

Did you ever wonder who
you could be at the zoo?
So many animals to choose,
So many things you could do!

You could be a monkey!
You'd swing from the trees.
You'd eat as many bananas
as you please.

Or…you could be a giraffe!
You'd stand so thin and tall,
Higher than the highest tree,
once and for all!

Or…you could be a bear!
You'd hide out in your den.
People would wait and watch
for you to come out again.

Or…you could be a zebra!
You'd wear stripes of black and white.
You'd pose for all of the cameras,
and you'd smile with all your might.

Or…you could be a tiger!
You'd play hide and seek.
No one would look exactly like you,
because your stripes are unique.

Or…you could be an elephant!
You'd have large, thin ears.
Your picture would be on the front
of all the souvenirs.

Or…you could be a lion!
You'd have a very thick mane.
You'd be the king of the jungle,
dare to enter your domain.

TIGERS
MONKEYS
ZEBRAS
ELEPHANTS
BEARS
GIRAFFES
LIONS
IMAGINATION

Did you ever wonder who
you could be at the zoo?
Next time you pass through,
your dreams could come true!

A Personal Note from the Author & Illustrator

Laurie never dreamed she would someday write a children's book. Instead, her childhood fantasy was to own a bakery and ice cream shop. However, after having a dream one night in January, 2013 that she could not ignore, Laurie knew that writing this book was something God wanted her to do. Shortly thereafter, she called her best friend, Jessica Barlup, and shared her up-beat and creative kid friendly poem and they began to collaborate.

Although Jessica has taught art to her students for nearly twelve years, she never considered herself to be an artist until more recently when Laurie invited her to illustrate her recently written story. Shortly after Laurie's proposition, Jessica began drawing several preliminary sketches that eventually evolved into the hand-painted acrylic illustrations that are pictured in this book. However, the pursuit of such an opportunity only became possible for her through the confidence Laurie displayed towards her artistic abilities and the overwhelming and endless support and love shown by her husband, Jason. This type of artistic endeavor is a first for both women and although it took countless hours of hard work and dedication to put it all together, Jessica would like to quote her friend Laurie by saying, "I feel this is only the beginning!" Looking ahead, Laurie and Jessica could not be more excited to share this book and are thankful for the dream that God shared with Laurie that one special night.

“SMILE! This book was made with love just for YOU!”

CPSIA information can be obtained
at www.ICGtesting.com
Printed in the USA
BVIC01n1111061013
332960BV00001B

* 9 7 8 1 6 1 2 4 4 1 7 5 7 *